A Child's Garden of Verses

By Robert Louis Stevenson

Illustrated by Alice and Martin Provensen

A GOLDEN BOOK · NEW YORK

The world is so full of a number of things,
I'm sure we should all be as happy as kings.

Cover art and interior illustrations copyright © 1951, renewed 1979 by Penguin Random House LLC.
All rights reserved. Published in the United States by Golden Books, an imprint of Random House Children's Books,
a division of Penguin Random House LLC, 1745 Broadway, New York, NY 10019, and in Canada by Penguin Random
House Canada Limited, Toronto. Originally published by Golden Press, Inc., New York, in 1951. Golden Books,
A Golden Book, and the G colophon are registered trademarks of Penguin Random House LLC.
randomhousekids.com
Educators and librarians, for a variety of teaching tools, visit us at
RHTeachersLibrarians.com
Library of Congress Control Number: 2016931106
ISBN 978-0-399-55537-4 (trade) — ISBN 978-0-399-55539-8 (ebook)
PRINTED IN CHINA
10 9 8 7 6 5 4 3 2 1

CONTENTS

# To Any Reader

As from the house your mother sees
You playing round the garden trees,
So you may see, if you will look
Through the windows of this book,
Another child, far, far away,
And in another garden, play.
But do not think you can at all,
By knocking on the window, call
That child to hear you. He intent
Is all on his play-business bent.
He does not hear; he will not look,
Nor yet be lured out of this book.
For, long ago, the truth to say,
He has grown up and gone away,
And it is but a child of air
That lingers in the garden there.

At the Seaside

When I was down beside the sea
A wooden spade they gave to me
    To dig the sandy shore.
My holes were empty like a cup,
In every hole the sea came up
    Till it could come no more.

My Shadow

I have a little shadow that goes in and out with me,
And what can be the use of him is more than I can see.
He is very, very like me from the heels up to the head;
And I see him jump before me, when I jump into my bed.

The funniest thing about him is the way he likes to grow—
Not at all like proper children, which is always very slow;
For he sometimes shoots up taller like an India-rubber ball,
And he sometimes gets so little that there's none of him at all.

He hasn't got a notion of how children ought to play,
And can only make a fool of me in every sort of way.
He stays so close beside me, he's a coward you can see;
I'd think shame to stick to nursie as that shadow sticks to me!

One morning, very early, before the sun was up,
I rose and found the shining dew on every buttercup;
But my lazy shadow, like an errant sleepyhead,
Had stayed at home behind me and was fast asleep in bed.

13

Autumn Fires

In the other gardens
    And all up the vale,
From the autumn bonfires
    See the smoke trail!

Pleasant summer over
    And all the summer flowers,
The red fire blazes,
    The gray smoke towers.

Sing a song of seasons!
    Something bright in all!
Flowers in the summer,
    Fires in the fall!

My Ship and I

O it's I that am the captain of a tidy little ship,
    Of a ship that goes a-sailing on the pond;
And my ship it keeps a-turning all around and all about;
But when I'm a little older, I shall find the secret out
    How to send my vessel sailing on beyond.

For I mean to grow as little as the dolly at the helm,
    And the dolly I intend to come alive;
And with him beside to help me, it's a-sailing I shall go,
It's a-sailing on the water, when the jolly breezes blow
    And the vessel goes a-divie-divie-dive.

O it's then you'll see me sailing through the rushes and the reeds,
    And you'll hear the water singing at the prow.
For beside the dolly sailor, I'm to voyage and explore,
To land upon the island where no dolly was before,
    And to fire the penny cannon in the bow.

The Wind

I saw you toss the kites on high
And blow the birds about the sky;
And all around I heard you pass,
Like ladies' skirts across the grass—
   O wind, a-blowing all day long,
   O wind, that sings so loud a song!

I saw the different things you did,
But always you yourself you hid.
I felt you push, I heard you call,
I could not see yourself at all—
   O wind, a-blowing all day long,
   O wind, that sings so loud a song!

O you that are so strong and cold,
O blower, are you young or old?
Are you a beast of field and tree,
Or just a stronger child than me?
   O wind, a-blowing all day long,
   O wind, that sings so loud a song!

Where Go the Boats?

Dark brown is the river,
  Golden is the sand.
It flows along forever,
  With trees on either hand.

Green leaves a-floating,
  Castles of the foam,
Boats of mine a-boating—
  Where will all come home?

On goes the river
   And out past the mill,
Away down the valley,
   Away down the hill.

Away down the river,
   A hundred miles or more,
Other little children
   Shall bring my boats ashore.

The Flowers

All the names I know from nurse:
Gardener's garters, Shepherd's purse,
Bachelor's buttons, Lady's smock,
And the Lady Hollyhock.

Fairy places, fairy things,
Fairy woods where the wild bee wings,
Tiny trees for tiny dames—
These must all be fairy names!

Tiny woods below whose boughs
Shady fairies weave a house;
Tiny tree-tops, rose or thyme,
Where the braver fairies climb!

Fair are grown-up people's trees,
But the fairest woods are these;
Where, if I were not so tall,
I should live for good and all.

The Cow

The friendly cow all red and white,
   I love with all my heart:
She gives me cream with all her might,
   To eat with apple-tart.

She wanders lowing here and there,
   And yet she cannot stray,
All in the pleasant open air,
   The pleasant light of day;

And blown by all the winds that pass
   And wet with all the showers,
She walks among the meadow grass
   And eats the meadow flowers.

Block City

What are you able to build with your blocks?
Castles and palaces, temples and docks.
Rain may keep raining, and others go roam,
But I can be happy and building at home.

Let the sofa be mountains, the carpet be sea,
There I'll establish a city for me:
A kirk and a mill and a palace beside,
And a harbor as well where my vessels may ride.

Great is the palace with pillar and wall,
A sort of a tower on the top of it all,
And steps coming down in an orderly way
To where my toy vessels lie safe in the bay.

This one is sailing and that one is moored:
Hark to the song of the sailors on board!
And see, on the steps of my palace, the kings
Coming and going with presents and things!

Now I have done with it, down let it go!
All in a moment the town is laid low.
Block upon block lying scattered and free,
What is there left of my town by the sea?

Yet as I saw it, I see it again,
The kirk and the palace, the ships and the men,
And as long as I live and where'er I may be,
I'll always remember my town by the sea.

Rain

The rain is raining all around,
It falls on field and tree,
It rains on the umbrellas here,
And on the ships at sea.

Windy Nights

Whenever the moon and stars are set,
   Whenever the wind is high,
All night long in the dark and wet,
   A man goes riding by.
Late in the night when the fires are out,
Why does he gallop and gallop about?

Whenever the trees are crying aloud,
   And ships are tossed at sea,
By, on the highway, low and loud,
   By at the gallop goes he.
By at the gallop he goes, and then
By he comes back at the gallop again.

From a Railway Carriage

Faster than fairies, faster than witches,
Bridges and houses, hedges and ditches;
And charging along like troops in a battle,
All through the meadows the horses and cattle:
All of the sights of the hill and the plain
Fly as thick as driving rain;
And ever again, in the wink of an eye,
Painted stations whistle by.

Here is a child who clambers and scrambles,
All by himself and gathering brambles;
Here is a tramp who stands and gazes;
And there is the green for stringing the daisies!
Here is a cart run away in the road
Lumping along with man and load;
And here is a mill and there is a river:
Each a glimpse and gone forever!

31

A Good Play

We built a ship upon the stairs
All made of the back-bedroom chairs,
And filled it full of sofa pillows
To go a-sailing on the billows.

We took a saw and several nails,
And water in the nursery pails;
And Tom said, "Let us also take
An apple and a slice of cake"—
Which was enough for Tom and me
To go a-sailing on, till tea.

We sailed along for days and days,
And had the very best of plays;
But Tom fell out and hurt his knee,
So there was no one left but me.

Foreign Lands

Up into the cherry tree
Who should climb but little me?
I held the trunk with both my hands
And looked abroad on foreign lands.

I saw the next-door garden lie,
Adorned with flowers, before my eye,
And many pleasant places more
That I had never seen before.

I saw the dimpling river pass
And be the sky's blue looking-glass;
The dusty roads go up and down
With people tramping into town.

If I could find a higher tree
Farther and farther I should see,
To where the grown-up river slips
Into the sea among the ships.

To where the roads on either hand
Lead onward into fairy land,
Where all the children dine at five,
And all the playthings come alive.

Looking Forward

When I am grown to man's estate
I shall be very proud and great,
And tell the other girls and boys
Not to meddle with my toys.

36

Nest Eggs

Birds all the sunny day
    Flutter and quarrel
Here in the arbor-like
    Tent of the laurel.

Here in the fork
    The brown nest is seated;
Four little blue eggs
    The mother keeps heated.

While we stand watching her,
    Staring like gabies,
Safe in each egg are the
    Bird's little babies.

Soon the frail eggs they shall
    Chip, and upspringing
Make all the April woods
    Merry with singing.

Younger than we are,
    O children, and frailer,
Soon in blue air they'll be,
    Singer and sailor.

We, so much older,
    Taller and stronger,
We shall look down on the
    Birdies no longer.

They shall go flying
    With musical speeches
High overhead in the
    Tops of the beeches.

In spite of our wisdom
    And sensible talking,
We on our feet must go
    Plodding and walking.

The Little Land

When at home alone I sit
And am very tired of it,
I have just to shut my eyes
To go sailing through the skies—
To go sailing far away
To the pleasant Land of Play;
To the fairy land afar
Where the Little People are;
Where the clover-tops are trees,
And the rain-pools are the seas,
And the leaves like little ships
Sail about on tiny trips;
And above the daisy tree
   Through the grasses,
High o'erhead the Bumble Bee
   Hums and passes.

In that forest to and fro
I can wander, I can go;
See the spider and the fly,
And the ants go marching by
Carrying parcels with their feet
Down the green and grassy street.
I can in the sorrel sit
Where the ladybird alit.
I can climb the jointed grass;
    And on high
See the greater swallows pass
    In the sky,
And the round sun rolling by
Heeding no such things as I.

40

Through that forest I can pass
Till, as in a looking-glass,
Humming fly and daisy tree
And my tiny self I see,
Painted very clear and neat
On the rain-pool at my feet.
Should a leaflet come to land
Drifting near to where I stand,
Straight I'll board that tiny boat,
Round the rain-pool sea to float.
Little thoughtful creatures sit
On the grassy coasts of it;
Little things with lovely eyes
See me sailing with surprise.

Some are clad in armor green—
(These have sure to battle been!)—
Some are pied with ev'ry hue,
Black and crimson, gold and blue;
Some have wings and swift are gone—
But they all look kindly on.
When my eyes I once again
Open, and see all things plain:
High bare walls, great bare floor;
Great big knobs on drawer and door;
Great big people perched on chairs,
Stitching tucks and mending tears,
Each a hill that I could climb,
And talking nonsense all the time—
    O dear me,
    That I could be
A sailor on the rain-pool sea,
A climber in the clover tree,
And just come back, a sleepy-head,
Late at night to go to bed.

The Whole Duty of Children

A child should always say what's true
And speak when he is spoken to,
And behave mannerly at table;
At least as far as he is able.

The Moon

The moon has a face like the clock in the hall;
She shines on thieves on the garden wall,
On streets and fields and harbor quays,
And birdies asleep in the forks of the trees.

44

The squalling cat and the squeaking mouse,
The howling dog by the door of the house,
The bat that lies in bed at noon,
All love to be out by the light of the moon.

But all of the things that belong to the day
Cuddle to sleep to be out of her way;
And flowers and children close their eyes
Till up in the morning the sun shall arise.

45

Singing

Of speckled eggs the birdie sings
And nests among the trees;
The sailor sings of ropes and things
In ships upon the seas.

The children sing in far Japan,
The children sing in Spain;
The organ with the organ man
Is singing in the rain.

The Dumb Soldier

When the grass was closely mown,
Walking on the lawn alone,
In the turf a hole I found,
And hid a soldier underground.

Spring and daisies came apace;
Grasses hide my hiding place;
Grasses run like a green sea
O'er the lawn up to my knee.

Under grass alone he lies,
Looking up with leaden eyes,
Scarlet coat and pointed gun,
To the stars and to the sun.

When the grass is ripe like grain,
When the scythe is stoned again,
When the lawn is shaven clear,
Then my hole shall reappear.

I shall find him, never fear,
I shall find my grenadier;
But for all that's gone and come,
I shall find my soldier dumb.

He has lived, a little thing,
In the grassy woods of spring;
Done, if he could tell me true,
Just as I should like to do.

He has seen the starry hours
And the springing of the flowers;
And the fairy things that pass
In the forests of the grass.

In the silence he has heard
Talking bee and ladybird,
And the butterfly has flown
O'er him as he lay alone.

Not a word will he disclose,
Not a word of all he knows.
I must lay him on the shelf,
And make up the tale myself.

The Swing

How do you like to go up in a swing,
   Up in the air so blue?
Oh, I do think it the pleasantest thing
   Ever a child can do!

Up in the air and over the wall,
   Till I can see so wide,
Rivers and trees and cattle and all
   Over the countryside—

Till I look down on the garden green,
   Down on the roof so brown—
Up in the air I go flying again,
   Up in the air and down!

The Hayloft

Through all the pleasant meadow-side
   The grass grew shoulder-high,
Till the shining scythes went far and wide
   And cut it down to dry.

These green and sweetly smelling crops
   They led in wagons home;
And they piled them here in mountaintops
   For mountaineers to roam.

Here is Mount Clear, Mount Rusty Nail,
   Mount Eagle and Mount High—
The mice that in these mountains dwell,
   No happier are than I!

Oh, what a joy to clamber there,
   Oh, what a place for play,
With the sweet, the dim, the dusty air,
   The happy hills of hay!

My Kingdom

Down by a shining water well
I found a very little dell,
　　No higher than my head.
The heather and the gorse about
In summer bloom were coming out,
　　Some yellow and some red.

I called the little pool a sea;
The little hills were big to me;
    For I am very small.
I made a boat, I made a town,
I searched the caverns up and down,
    And named them one and all.

And all about was mine, I said,
The little sparrows overhead,
    The little minnows too.
This was the world and I was king;
For me the bees came by to sing,
    For me the swallows flew.

I played there were no deeper seas,
Nor any wider plains than these,
    Nor other kings than me.
At last I heard my mother call
Out from the house at evenfall,
    To call me home to tea.

And I must rise and leave my dell,
And leave my dimpled water well,
    And leave my heather blooms.
Alas! and as my home I neared
How very big my nurse appeared.
    How great and cool the rooms!

The Land of Counterpane

When I was sick and lay a-bed,
I had two pillows at my head,
And all my toys beside me lay
To keep me happy all the day.

And sometimes for an hour or so
I watched my leaden soldiers go,
With different uniforms and drills,
Among the bed-clothes, through the hills;

And sometimes sent my ships in fleets
All up and down among the sheets;
Or brought my trees and houses out,
And planted cities all about.

I was the giant great and still
That sits upon the pillow-hill,
And sees before him, dale and plain,
The pleasant land of counterpane.

Time to Rise

A birdie with a yellow bill
Hopped upon the window sill,
Cocked his shining eye and said:
"Ain't you 'shamed, you sleepy-head!"

Fairy Bread

Come up here, O dusty feet!
  Here is fairy bread to eat.
Here in my retiring room,
  Children, you may dine
On the golden smell of broom
  And the shade of the pine;
And when you have eaten well,
Fairy stories hear and tell.

Farewell to the Farm

The coach is at the door at last;
The eager children, mounting fast
And kissing hands, in chorus sing:
Goodbye, goodbye, to everything!

To house and garden, field and lawn,
The meadow-gates we swung upon,
To pump and stable, tree and swing,
Goodbye, goodbye, to everything!

And fare you well for evermore,
O ladder at the hayloft door,
O hayloft where the cobwebs cling,
Goodbye, goodbye, to everything!

Crack goes the whip, and off we go;
The trees and houses smaller grow;
Last, round the woody turn we swing;
Goodbye, goodbye, to everything!

Pirate Story

Three of us afloat in the meadow by the swing,
   Three of us aboard in the basket on the lea.
Winds are in the air, they are blowing in the spring,
   And waves are on the meadow like the waves there are at sea.

Where shall we adventure, today that we're afloat,
   Wary of the weather and steering by a star?
Shall it be to Africa, a-steering of the boat,
   To Providence, or Babylon, or off to Malabar?

Hi! but here's a squadron a-rowing on the sea—
Cattle on the meadow a-charging with a roar!
Quick, and we'll escape them, they're as mad as they can be,
The wicket is the harbor and the garden is the shore.

My Bed Is a Boat

My bed is like a little boat;
    Nurse helps me in when I embark;
She girds me in my sailor's coat
    And starts me in the dark.

At night, I go on board and say
    Good night to all my friends on shore;
I shut my eyes and sail away
    And see and hear no more.

And sometimes things to bed I take,
   As prudent sailors have to do:
Perhaps a slice of wedding cake,
   Perhaps a toy or two.

All night across the dark we steer;
   But when the day returns at last,
Safe in my room, beside the pier,
   I find my vessel fast.

The Land of Nod

From breakfast on through all the day
At home among my friends I stay;
But every night I go abroad
Afar into the land of Nod.

All by myself I have to go,
With none to tell me what to do—
All alone beside the streams
And up the mountain-sides of dreams.

The strangest things are there for me,
Both things to eat and things to see,
And many frightening sights abroad
Till morning in the land of Nod.

Try as I like to find the way,
I never can get back by day,
Nor can remember plain and clear
The curious music that I hear.

The Lamplighter

My tea is nearly ready and the sun has left the sky.
It's time to take the window to see Leerie going by;
For every night at teatime and before you take your seat,
With lantern and with ladder he comes posting up the street.

Now Tom would be a driver and Maria go to sea,
And my papa's a banker and as rich as he can be;
But I, when I am stronger and can choose what I'm to do,
O Leerie, I'll go round at night and light the lamps with you!

For we are very lucky, with a lamp before the door,
And Leerie stops to light it as he lights so many more;
And O! before you hurry by with ladder and with light,
O Leerie, see a little child and nod to him tonight!

Escape at Bedtime

The lights from the parlor and kitchen shone out
    Through the blinds and the windows and bars;
And high overhead and all moving about,
    There were thousands of millions of stars.

There ne'er were such thousands of leaves on a tree,
    Nor of people in church or the Park,
As the crowds of the stars that looked down upon me,
    And that glittered and winked in the dark.

The Dog, and the Plough, and the Hunter, and all,
    And the star of the sailor, and Mars,
These shone in the sky, and the pail by the wall
    Would be half full of water and stars.

They saw me at last, and they chased me with cries,
    And they soon had me packed into bed;
But the glory kept shining and bright in my eyes,
    And the stars going round in my head.

Bed in Summer

In winter I get up at night
And dress by yellow candlelight.
In summer, quite the other way,
I have to go to bed by day.

I have to go to bed and see
The birds still hopping on the tree,
Or hear the grown-up people's feet
Still going past me in the street.

And does it not seem hard to you,
When all the sky is clear and blue,
And I should like so much to play,
To have to go to bed by day?